THE MYSTERIOUS WORLD OF COSENTINO

After so many years, to finally see the characters and worlds inside my head come to life is truly a dream come true. I dedicate this book to all those boys and girls who are reluctant readers. I hope this book is the key to unlock a hidden passion to read and that you find the magic within.
—COS

For Cos—and all the other misfits who do amazing things
—Jack Heath

For Amanda, who encourages and believes in me each and every day
—James Hart

First American Edition 2018
Kane Miller, A Division of EDC Publishing
PO Box 470663
Tulsa, OK 74147-0663

Text & illustrations copyright © Scholastic Australia, 2017.
Text by Cosentino with Jack Heath.
Illustrations by James Hart.

Internal images: p45 and various pages, Stars © Alisovna/Creative MarketFirst

First published by Scholastic Australia division of Scholastic Australia Pty Limited in 2017
This edition published under license from Scholastic Australia Pty Limited

www.kanemiller.com
www.edcpub.com
www.usbornebooksandmore.com

Library of Congress Control Number: 2017958232

Printed and bound in the United States of America

1 2 3 4 5 6 7 8 9 10

ISBN: 978-1-61067-749-3

THE MYSTERIOUS WORLD OF COSENTINO

THE MISSING ACE

By

THE GRAND ILLUSIONIST

WITH JACK HEATH

ILLUSTRATED BY JAMES HART

Kane Miller
A DIVISION OF EDC PUBLISHING

The Runaway Ace

The snakes **hissed** and **squirmed** in the pit. There were hundreds of them, all tangled up like spaghetti. Their scales and eyes shone in the darkness as they crawled over one another. Deadly venom dripped from their

ENORMOUS FANGS.

Cosentino, the Grand Illusionist, and his best friend, Locki, stared down into the snake pit. Locki looked nervous.

"The snakes aren't venomous, right?" Locki asked.

"Wrong," Cos said cheerfully. "The guy who sold them to me said one bite could make my heart explode!"

OK, so how does this trick work again?

It's simple.

Hisssssssssss

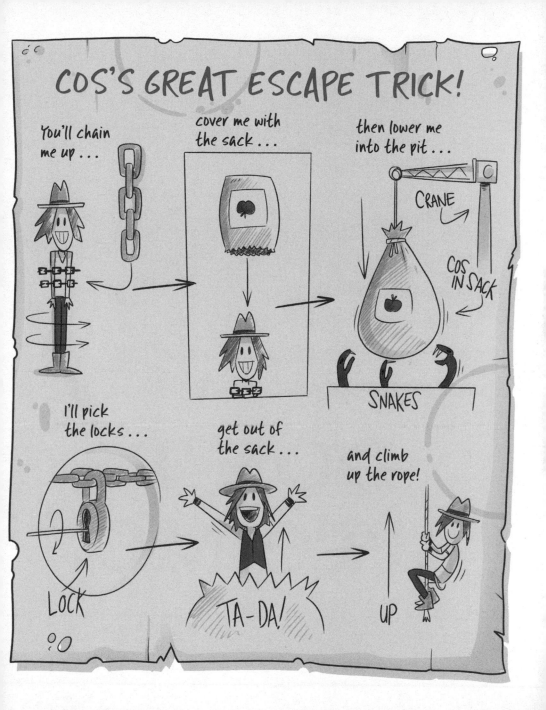

"It doesn't look simple. Are you sure you can pull it off?" Locki wondered.

"I thought you were supposed to have nerves of steel!" Cos exclaimed.

"No, I'm only *made* of steel," Locki said. "Those snakes are deadly!"

"Keep your dial on, Locki," Cos said, warming up with a hamstring stretch. "I'll use a clarinet to **charm** the snakes so they

DON'T BiTe Me."

LOCKI

Cos's partner at Copperpot Theater, Coppertown
Abilities: Lock-picking

Locki was a padlock who could open just about anything. He and Cos had grown up together, practicing magic tricks and escapes, back when Coppertown was a nice place to live. The two friends had put on thousands of shows at Cos's Copperpot Theater.

The theater had become run-down in recent years, but it was beloved by the residents of Coppertown, and was Cos's home.

11

COSENTINO

MAGICIAN AT COPPERPOT THEATER, COPPERTOWN
ABILITIES: ESCAPE, SLEIGHT OF HAND, TELEKINESIS, ILLUSION

Some of the stunts Cos performed on the Copperpot Theater stage were very dangerous and without Locki's help, Cos would have been burned or buried alive or drowned long ago. But this time, Locki wasn't sure his special lock-picking abilities would be much help if Cos fell into the pit of venomous snakes. Even Cos's own magical skills wouldn't be able to save him from that. If Cos died, Locki would be **devastated**.

Locki took a deep breath. "I trust you, Cos. But

how will the audience see what's going on in the pit?"

"Oh." Cos looked around the empty theater. Locki was right. The pit was in the middle of the stage, and the stage was tall. Even the highest rows of seats wouldn't be able to see the actual snakes.

"We could use the mirror from the vanishing trick," Locki suggested. "Hang it over the stage at an angle. Or we could—"

THE DOOR BURST OPEN.

"Who are you?" Locki demanded.

**I'm Ace.
The King's army
is after me!**

Cos felt his heartbeat get faster.

**WE HAVE THE BUILDING
SURROUNDED!**

A shrill voice echoed from outside the theater.

COME OUT WITH YOUR HANDS UP!

Ace looked terrified.

"I used to be in the army. I was one of them,"
Ace explained. "But I escaped . . ."

The King's Army of 52 was made up of spades, clubs, hearts and diamonds. The soldiers were **strong** and **fast** and had **magical abilities**. They had been hypnotized by the evil King to obey his orders without question. Everyone in Magicland feared them.

"WE KNOW YOU'RE iN THERE!"

a booming voice said.

"It's Hollow!" Ace squeaked.

"He's found me!"

HOLLOW

King's henchman at Silver Castle, Silver City
Abilities: Can smell magic

Hollow was a magic wand who worked for the King, hunting down magical objects.

Magic—not tricks, *real* magic—was illegal in Coppertown.

The King wanted to make sure no one could lead a rebellion against him, so he had **banned all spells** outside of Silver City when he took the throne there, six years ago.

If Hollow found the **spell book** Cos kept hidden in the attic, Cos and Locki would be in **deep trouble**.

"How many soldiers are with him?" Cos asked.

"I don't know," Ace said.

"Five," said a voice.

Ace looked around. "Who said that?"

"Oh," Cos said, "that was Snuggles."

SNUGGLES

Lettuce disposal expert in Cos's hat
Abilities: Appearing and disappearing, heightened senses

A white rabbit popped her head out from Cos's hat. Her nose twitched.

"Five soldiers," she said again, pointing her paw at Ace.

"They smell like you. No offense, but I believe in calling a spade a spade."

"None taken," Ace said.

Snuggles had an amazing sense of smell.

Unfortunately, she mostly used it to seek out lettuce, and left flakes of it in Cos's hat.

"YOU HAVE THIRTY SECONDS TO COME OUT!"

Hollow shouted,

"OR WE'RE COMING IN!"

"Please!" Ace whispered.

Cos couldn't let Hollow search the building. But he couldn't make Ace go outside. If Ace had escaped from the King's army, who knew what the King would do to him?

A plan began to form in his mind.

"Hide inside this." Cos threw the sack from his escape trick at Ace. "Locki! Where's the Professor?"

Professor Camouflage was a lizard with the ability to change his appearance.

PROFESSOR CAMOUFLAGE
·•·

CELEBRITY IMPERSONATOR AT SIEGFRIED ALLEY, COPPERTOWN (SINCE ESCAPING FROM THE ROYAL ZOO)
ABILITIES: CAN DISGUISE HIMSELF AS ANYTHING

At the moment he was the same color as the dusty curtains hanging beside the stage.

He'd been there all along.

Hello!

"Can I be of assistance?" he said.

"Professor," Cos said. "Can you lead the King's men away from here?"

With pleasure.

ALL OF a SUDDEN . . .

WHOOSH!

HiS PEBBLED SKiN TURNED GRAY

HiS FEET STRETCHED iNTO COWBOY BOOTS,

AND iN SECONDS BANG

HE LOOKED JUST LiKE ACE!

"Ten seconds!" Hollow shouted from outside. He sounded very **angry** now.

"Locki," Cos said, "go open the door."

Locki **jumped** off the stage and **ran** up the aisle.

Cos turned to Ace, who was now crouched inside the rough brown sack.

"I'm **really, really sorry** about this," Cos said.

If you keep still, they probably won't bite.

Then he PUSHED Ace into the SNAKE PIT!

HOLLOW'S HUNT

The door opened. Light spilled over the dusty chairs and tattered carpet of Cos's theater.

Cos shielded his eyes as Hollow pushed past Locki and strode in, followed by two soldiers. The three others stayed outside.

Hollow was tall and **imposing**. He wore a fancy vest and a monocle.

He peered around the theater and turned up his nose.

"How . . . quaint," he sneered.
Then he sniffed.

I smell spelldust!

Spelldust was the glittering
substance which appeared in the air
when a spell was cast. Most people
could only see it, but Hollow could
smell it for months afterward. This
was why the King had chosen him to
hunt down illegal magic users.

"No spells here," Cos said.

Hollow saw him. "You," he said.
"You own this place?"

Cos bowed. "I'm **Cosentino, the
Grand Illusionist**. At your service."

Sniff
Sniff

"Are you aware that magic is against the law?"
Hollow said.

This wasn't exactly true. The King had made
sure magic was still legal in Silver City because
his palace was there.

He wanted to keep eating **MAGIC FOOD** which **NEVER RAN OUT**,

using **MAGIC BATH WATER** which **NEVER GOT COLD**,

and riding in **MAGIC TAXIS** which **ARRIVED BEFORE THEY LEFT**.

But in Coppertown, **ALL MAGIC** was banned.

Cos thought this was **unfair**. Magic should belong to everyone, not just the lucky few who lived in Silver City. But it wouldn't be smart to say that in front of Hollow.

"I know magic is banned. I perform *illusions*," Cos said.

"The sign outside says you're a magician," challenged Hollow.

"That sign is out of date. My illusions may look like magic, but they are actually tricks. Just like this."

He took off his hat and pulled Snuggles out.

Hollow was so surprised his monocle fell out.

"Great job, Snuggles," Cos said. He put her back in the hat, and put the hat on his head. "I'd like to change the 'magician' sign, but it's very high up and magic stepladders are banned."

"Why not use a regular stepladder?" Hollow growled.

Cos scratched his chin, stalling for time. "Magic stepladders don't wobble. I suppose we could steady a normal ladder with a—"

Hollow walked closer and jabbed Cos in the chest with a bony finger. "Enough talk," he hissed. **"Where's the spade?"**

31

"What spade?" Cos asked. He looked at Locki. "Locki, have you seen any spades hanging around?"

Locki frowned. "I don't think so."

"Search the building," Hollow snapped at the two soldiers.

When the soldiers started **smashing** through the seats with their big fists, Cos winced. His theater was old and small, but he loved it—and now it was being destroyed.

Hollow walked down the aisle and then leaped up onto the stage.

Hollow **glared** at them both. "So I see. But what's in the sack?"

Cos hoped Ace would keep still inside the bag. "More snakes," he said.

"Snake food," Locki said at exactly the same moment.

"More food for the snakes," Cos clarified. "Exactly." He waved an arm across the pit. "Feel free to go down there and have a look."

One of the snakes gave Hollow a hungry look, its forked tongue lashing the air.

Hollow pointed at Locki.
"*You* go down there," he said.
"Bring the sack to me."

Locki looked alarmed.

"I'll do it," Cos said. He
couldn't put Locki in danger.

"You just said you
perform tricks for a living,"
Hollow said. "I won't be
tricked by you. I want the
padlock to go down there
instead. Now go, before I arrest you both."

Cos looked at Locki, worried. People who got
arrested by Hollow were sent to THE ARCADE—
the King's special dungeon. There were rumors
that the King had cast a spell on The Arcade, so it
was always night inside.

The jailer was said to be a MAD CREATURE, neither human nor animal.

These were just stories. No one knew for sure, since no one who entered THE ARCADE ever came out again.

But from time to time, Cos had been told,
strange noises echoed out from the entrance.

OFF-KEY CARNIVAL MUSIC.

GOTCHA 3

3

DEATH RIDE

DUNGEON OF D

insert coi

HUNGRY GROWLS.

TERRIFYING SCREAMS.

Cos had to quickly come up with an excuse to distract Hollow, but then a movement on the roof caught his eye.

Hollow whirled around in time to see the Professor, camouflaged as Ace, drop to the floor of the theater in front of the door. The big soldiers lunged toward him, but they were too slow. The Professor leaped out of reach and sprinted out the door into the street.

AFTER HIM!

The soldiers chased after him.

"This isn't over," Hollow snarled. Then he ran up the aisle after them, leaving Locki and Cos alone on the stage.

SNAKE CHARMING

"OK," Cos said finally. "They're gone."

The brown sack wriggled at the bottom of the snake pit. The snakes **hissed** angrily, yellow eyes gleaming. There were **BROWN SNAKES**, **TIGER SNAKES**, **PUFF ADDERS**, **cobras**, **VIPERS**, **kraits**, **taipans**—even a **Massive anaconda**, coiled in the corner like a truck tire. Ankle-deep water was teeming with sea snakes.

One bite from those vicious snakes could be deadly.

"Keep still," Cos told Ace. "We'll get you out."

"How?" Locki whispered.

"Trust me," Cos said. "I'm a magician."

He grabbed his clarinet and crouched down at the edge of the pit.

"**Are you watching closely?**" he asked Locki.

Get me out of here!

Without waiting for Locki to reply, Cos jumped down into the pit.

Startled by the sudden movement, the snakes slithered out of the way as he landed with a **splash**.

Cos ignored the fluttering of his heart. *Stay calm*, he told himself. *They can smell **fear***.

The snakes swam and crawled back toward

Cos. A black mamba **bared** its fearsome teeth.
A rattlesnake **shook** its tail. The sound sent
shivers down Cos's spine.

As the snakes converged on him, he put the
clarinet to his lips, took a deep breath, and blew.

The clarinet made an embarrassing

SQUEAK!

The snakes
stopped moving.
They watched
Cos, confused.

Cos blew again. The clarinet honked like a goose choking on a chunk of bread.

The snakes all rose, slowly. Soon they were standing on their tails.

Cos blew another note.

The snakes started swaying from side to side.

MAGIC SECRET UNLOCKED

Cos was a terrible musician. Fortunately, the snakes were deaf. They couldn't hear the instrument—they could only see it moving. This was the secret of snake charming: they would follow the bobbing of the clarinet, **hypnotized**.

Cos waded over to the sack, still making **ugly sounds** with the clarinet as he waved it around. He tore the sack open with one hand.

Ace squinted up at the stage lights above the pit. Then he saw the snakes.

"**Snakes!**" he yelled, unnecessarily.

"Locki," Cos called, "throw down the rope!" Then he stuck the clarinet back in his mouth. He kept waving it from side to side as he and Ace tiptoed toward the side of the pit.

The snakes were getting **bolder**. A copperhead

lay down and slithered closer to
Ace's legs.

Locki lowered a rough brown rope
into the pit. "**Climb up!**" he shouted.

A big cobra twisted itself into a
squiggly shape, ready to leap at Ace's
ankles.

Cos spat out the clarinet. "You first," he
said to the spade. "**Quick!**"

Ace scrambled up the rope. As soon as he was
out of the way, the cobra turned to look at Cos. Its
huge body was like a **coiled spring**.

Cos grabbed the bottom of the rope and started

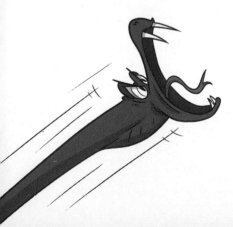

climbing. The cobra **pounced**,
massive fangs bared as it **shot**
through the air toward Cos's
kicking feet—

AND SLAMMED FACE-FIRST INTO THE WALL.

Locki had pulled the rope up just in time. Cos hauled himself out of the pit and onto the stage. He lay on the dirty boards, breathing heavily.

Locki was hopping from foot to foot with excitement. "You did it!" he cried.

"We did it," Cos said. "I just wish we had an audience. A performance like that would have made us famous throughout Magicland."

Ace sat up. "Your music was awful," he said. "How did you charm the snakes?"

"Can you keep a secret?" Cos asked.

Ace nodded.

"So can I," Cos said.

THE CHASE

Hollow sprinted through the marketplace, pushing merchants and customers aside. If the spade got away, the King would be **furious**.

Or maybe not. It was hard to predict the mood of the King, who was often in **two minds** about something. Possibly because he had two heads.

Either way, Hollow wanted to know how the spade had escaped from the King's army. It was supposed to be **impossible** to do. Every soldier had been hypnotized by the King himself.

Hollow turned a corner and kept running past crowded stalls, his soldiers following closely behind. He **hated** coming to Coppertown. It was much dirtier and smellier than Silver City.

He supposed it was because they couldn't use magic to clean things. Many of these shops had sold magic items before

The GREAT DISENCHANTMENT,

when the King outlawed magic. Now they had to sell items strictly for non-magic uses only.

COPPERPOT THEATER
Rug Shop
That rug is made of the finest wool, sir, just watch out—it bites.
Cauldrons! Get ex-magic cauldrons here, only ten copper pieces each! Great for casseroles!
HOT POT CAULDRONS

Lamp Shop
PRICES YOU'D WISH FOR
Did you see that angry wand run past?
Seems fishy.
That reminds me, I'm hungry.
Ooh, silver rings! And top hats! Perfect for the costume party, don't you think, Harry?
SILVER MAGIC RINGS
MAGIC TOP HATS
Perfume Shop

Hollow couldn't see any **spelldust** in the air, but he didn't have time to slow down and make sure no one was breaking the law. He was too busy following the Professor, who had ducked into an alleyway up ahead.

THAT WAY! GET HiM!

The five soldiers ran into the alley, bellowing battle cries. Their boots left patterns in the dust.

Hollow entered the alley and looked around. He saw some overturned trash cans, a parked wagon and a crow pecking at the dirt.

The spade had vanished . . .

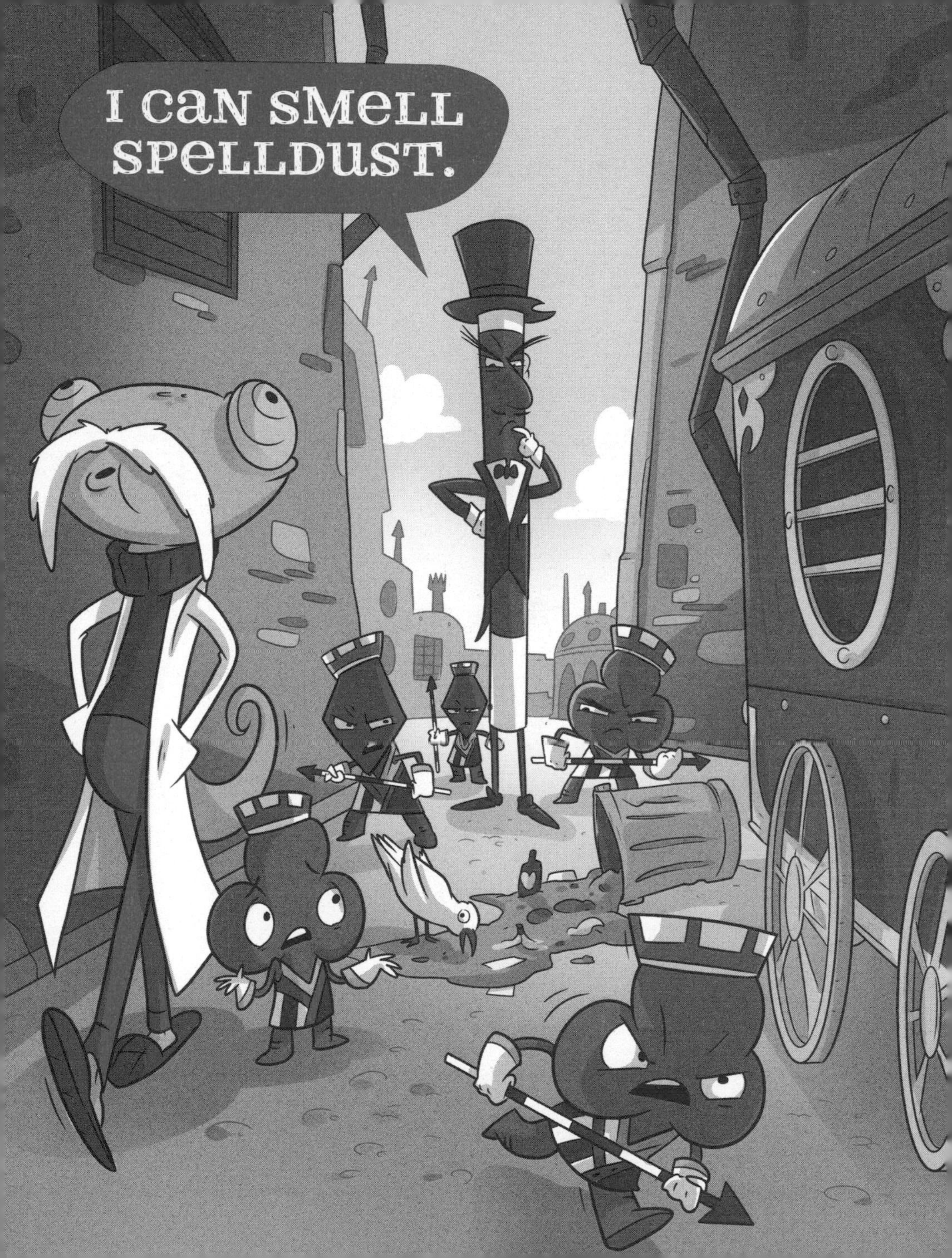
I CAN SMELL SPELLDUST.

Something magical had just happened, but Hollow wasn't sure what. The spade he was looking for didn't have the power of invisibility, teleportation or shapeshifting. Ace's power was **transformation**—he could turn creatures and objects into other things for a short period of time.

And yet he was gone.

Hollow kicked at the dust, grinding his teeth. This wasn't over.

"What do we do, boss?" one of the soldiers asked.

"That magician knew something," Hollow said. "I'm going to find out what."

SHARK TANK

"Ladies and gentlemen," Cos said to the Copperpot Theater audience. "This will be my last illusion tonight, possibly ever, since it's very **dangerous**. I could be badly injured, or even killed."

He paused to let the words sink in.

The theater was close to full. By banning magic, the King had made illusions more popular than ever. People came from all over Coppertown to watch Cos's shows.

A young woman in a gray cloak sat two rows back from the front, her face shadowed by a hood. Cos could only see her wide blue eyes. He winked at her.

"So," he said, "if you don't want to see me die, now is your chance to leave."

No one left the room.

"You're all happy to watch me die?" Cos said. "OK then. Good to know."

Nervous laughter echoed through the theater.

Cos hadn't wanted to perform the snake escape tonight—not after he and Ace had nearly died in the snake pit this morning. But Ace had given him the chance to perform a **different** stunt. Cos had asked him to change a big wooden crate into a glass-walled box. Ace had also transformed three of the snakes into sharks.

ACE

SOLDIER IN THE ARMY OF 52,
SILVER CASTLE, SILVER CITY
ABILITIES: TRANSFORMATION

The spade seemed very kind, which explained how he had escaped from the King's army. The King's hypnosis only worked on people who were cruel, or selfish, or cowardly. Ace had a clear conscience, so he had been able to run away.

Cos walked over to the big glass box, which was covered by a red sheet. He pulled the sheet off.

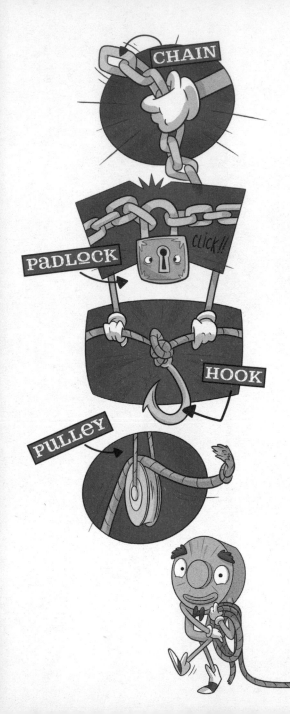

Locki walked onto the stage holding a steel **chain** and a **rope**. He wrapped the chain around Cos several times, holding his legs together and pinning his arms to his sides. He **padlocked** the links to one another and tied the rope to a **hook** behind Cos's neck. He threw the other end over a **pulley** above the tank.

"**I will be hanging by a burning rope over the shark tank**," Cos announced. "If I pick these three locks and escape from the chain before the rope snaps, I will be able to swing to safety. If I don't, I will drop into the tank. I hope the sharks are friendly."

There was no laughter this time. The crowd stared in **horror**—but also fascination. Cos had seen this many times. People didn't want to watch, but couldn't bring themselves to look away.

Locki struck a match and touched it to the rope, which had been dunked in kerosene. The **flames raced** up the rope. Cos felt the back of his head get hot.

"Lift me up!" he commanded.

He was already wriggling. The chain wasn't quite as tight as it looked. Cos just had to get one arm free, and then he could use the paper clip hidden in his hand to pick the first lock.

The burning rope went tight. Cos was lifted into the air. Soon he was above the shark tank. The sharks were swimming back and forth right under his feet. As snakes, they hadn't had a chance to kill him. Now they wanted **revenge**, and they were keen to try out all their new teeth.

Cos managed to push his hand through a gap between the chains. He unfolded the paper clip and jammed one end into a padlock.

The burning rope **crackled** above his head. Cos could already smell the smoke.

The padlock popped open. It hit the stage with a

THUNK!

Now that the chain was looser, Cos could get his whole arm free. He wriggled around until he found the second padlock and started picking it.

The fire was getting hotter. The rope was coming apart. Stray fibers rained down around him, **fizzling** and **hissing** as they hit the water below.

KACHUNK!

The second padlock was unlocked. Only one to go.

The paper clip slipped out of Cos's hand. There was a small splash as it hit the water.

Someone in the audience **screamed**, which set off someone else.

NOOO!

Uh-oh!

Aaaghh!

Eeeeek!

Cos struggled, trying to free himself from the chains. But with the last padlock still closed, he couldn't get his legs free.

THE BURNING ROPE SNAPPED.

Cos fell for a heart-stopping second before he hit the water—

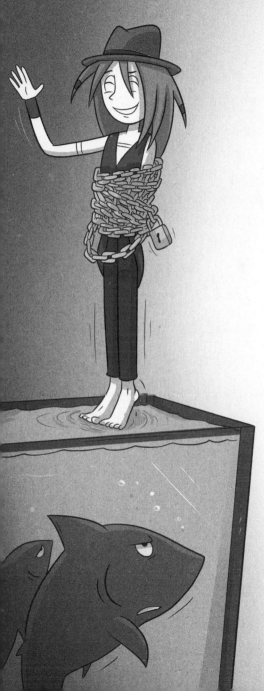

But he didn't sink.
Shocked murmurs
filled the crowd as Cos
stood on top of the water!

It was like he was
wearing floating shoes,
except the audience
could clearly see his bare
feet. It was impossible.

The sharks chased
each other's tails inches
below his toes.

The audience exploded
into applause. Cheers
and shrieks filled the
theater.

MAGIC SECRET UNLOCKED

Cos was actually standing on a pane of
glass concealed a couple of inches
beneath the surface of the water.
There was a spare paper clip in his mouth
which he used to pick the last lock and
unwind the chain.

Cos took a bow. There was an invisible hole in
the glass floor just in front of him. He dropped
the chain through the hole so the audience could
watch it sink. The sharks **nipped** at the chain.
The clapping got even louder.

"**Cosentino!**" a voice shouted.

Cos shielded his eyes from the stage lights.
Hollow was striding down the aisle flanked by two
soldiers.

The audience fell silent. When the King's army came to Coppertown, it always meant trouble. The woman in the hooded cloak looked especially worried. Cos wondered what she had to hide.

"So nice to see you again, Mr. Hello," Cos said.

"It's Hollow," the magic wand snapped. He pointed at Cos, who still appeared to be floating on top of the water.

ARREST THAT MAN!

69

Then everything happened at once.

The crowd scrambled
out of their seats as
the soldiers barreled
down the aisle toward
Cos, who did a backflip
off the shark tank and
landed on the stage.

Locki sprinted toward the tank with an ax.
(They always kept an ax handy in case a water
escape went wrong.)

"**Run, Cos!**" he cried. Then he **slammed** the ax into the tank.

The glass **shattered**.

Screams filled the air as water poured off the stage and onto the seats. The soldiers, who had been climbing up to the stage, were knocked down by the **flying sharks**, which immediately changed back into snakes.

Shocked and confused, the soldiers wrestled with the deadly snakes as the audience rushed toward the exits.

IT WAS PANDEMONIUM.

COS FLED.

Soon Cos was standing at the **edge** of the
rooftop of his theater. He couldn't see any
soldiers—they must all be inside, looking for
him. If he could get down to street level, he could
lure the soldiers away **before they found Ace
hiding in the attic . . .**

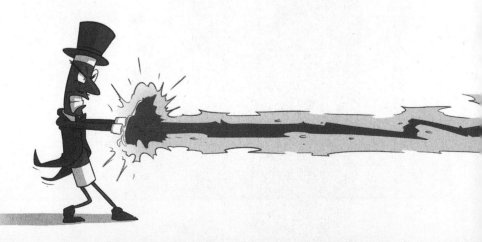

And the illegal **spell book**.

If Hollow saw that, Cos was **doomed**.
He would spend the rest of his life in
The Arcade.

It was too far to jump. The fall would kill him
instantly.

MAGIC SECRET UNLOCKED

Cos had once been a "human fly"—a performer who climbed tall buildings without any equipment. Cos had drilled **invisible finger holes** in the walls of his theater so he could perform this trick.

He crouched down, looking for the first row of finger holes. If he could find them, he would be able to climb down to safety.

"Freeze! IN THE NaMe of THE KiNG!" Hollow yelled as he emerged out of the rooftop trapdoor, puffing.

Cos spotted the finger holes. He reached down—

Then Hollow hit him with a blast of magic, and the whole world went black.

SILVER CITY

Cos woke up inside a horse-drawn carriage. His head was spinning. Hollow had hit him with a lot of magic—the sort which could stop a person's heart, or fry their brains. Cos was lucky to be alive.

The carriage doors were bolted from the outside, so Cos couldn't pick the locks. The windows were barred. He thought about trying to kick through the floor and escape onto the road, but he would probably be **crushed** by the wheels.

Magic crackled outside, and the wheels of the carriage began to lift off the ground. The carriage rose higher and higher, **glistening spelldust** swirling around it. Cos peered out the window and could see Silver City up ahead—an enormous box, floating in the clouds.

The whole city was inside the box, connected to the ground only by a thin ladder of hovering steps. The walls of the box were mirrored, so the city seemed to go on forever.

Once Cos was inside, there would be no escape.

Two guards stood outside the gates, making sure no Coppertown residents could sneak in. They saluted Hollow as he drove the carriage into Silver City.

Inside the gates, the streets were paved with silver. Magic lights shone from behind the windows of huge houses.

Cos couldn't help but marvel at the floating objects and dazzling lights. Seeing magic, real magic, made him feel like a little boy again. The world seemed full of wonder. Anything was possible.

The royal palace was a silver tower, surrounded by mist. Gargoyles jutted out from the edges of the roof. One of them turned to watch as the carriage approached. Cos felt like it was looking right at him.

"Well, you're sunk," said a voice from inside Cos's fedora.

"**Snuggles!** I forgot you were in there."

The rabbit popped her head out. Flakes of lettuce were stuck to her fluffy chin. Cos had no idea how she had smuggled food in there without him knowing.

"Obviously," Snuggles said. "I know you're headed toward certain **death**, but did you really have to take me with you?"

Cos scratched her behind the ears.

Sorry, Snuggles. Don't worry, I'm a magician. I'll get us out of this.

Snuggles looked doubtful. "Uh-huh. Well, if the King decides to **burn** you alive or **drown** you or **bury** you, make sure you're not wearing the hat."

She disappeared back into the darkness of Cos's hat.

"Thanks for your support, Snuggles," Cos grumbled. But she was right. He didn't have a plan, and he was running out of time to create one.

The carriage rolled up the driveway—which was pebbled with tiny nuggets of silver—toward the palace. When it crossed the drawbridge and stopped, Hollow opened the carriage door.

"But of course," Cos beamed, as though it had been a polite request, and climbed out.

Hollow pushed Cos through a set of big double doors, past several armed guards and up five flights of stairs. Eventually Hollow opened another door and Cos found himself in a huge chamber. Candles burned in chandeliers high overhead. The floor was checkered like a chessboard.

The lords and ladies of Magicland were dressed in **puffy** silk clothes and **sparkling** jewelry. Because magic was legal here, they could conjure up whatever clothes or possessions they wanted, so long as they didn't try to outshine the King. They all had **perfect** teeth thanks to magical dentistry, and **glowing** skin thanks to magical moisturizer.

When they saw Cos, with his bare feet and plain trousers, the lords and ladies backed away as though he had an **infectious** disease.

A waiter walked past carrying a platter of fruit and pastries. Cos took an apple and tucked it into his sleeve so quickly that nobody saw him do it.

A huge rabbit, easily twice as big as Cos, was standing right beside the King.

The King himself was seated on an enormous silver throne. The stories were true—the King had two heads, one beneath the other. Neither of them looked pleased to see Cos.

THE KING OF DIAMONDS

KING OF MAGICLAND, SILVER CASTLE, SILVER CITY
ABILITIES: HYPNOTISM

"Hollow, who is this?" one of the King's heads bellowed.

"This man was found performing magic in Coppertown, your majesty," Hollow said.

"Your majesty, I use no magic," Cos said. "I am Cosentino, the Grand Illusionist. I perform tricks, like so." He opened his hands, showing them to be empty. He waggled his fingers, then he reached out and plucked an apple from the air.

MAGIC SECRET UNLOCKED

After hiding the apple up his sleeve, Cos only needed to let it fall into his palm.

This was a simple trick, but the crowd looked horrified.

Cos tossed the apple to a nearby man, who dropped it like a hot coal.

"Magic is illegal for common Coppertowners!" the King roared.

"Indeed it is, your majesty," Cos said quickly. "I would **never use real magic**. This is mere illusion. Note the lack of spelldust in the air. And your servant, Mr. Jello—"

"It's Hollow," the magic wand growled.

Cos ignored him. "He can sense magic, yes? I'm sure he'll tell you I didn't use any."

The King looked expectantly at Hollow.

"No magic," Hollow grumbled.

"Pretend magic still makes a mockery of our laws," the King said.

OFF WITH HIS HEAD!

The crowd gasped. The King waved his hand like a puppeteer, and the enormous rabbit reached behind the throne and picked up a broadsword with one muscular arm. Then it bared its huge teeth and marched toward Cos, the sword raised.

FLEX

KING'S BODYGUARD, SILVER CASTLE, SILVER CITY
ABILITIES: SUPERSTRONG

Cos backed away, his heart racing. It looked like the King had **hypnotized** the giant rabbit—he could control anyone with even a drop of evil in their heart. Cos wouldn't be able to talk the rabbit out of killing him.

The King made a chopping motion with one hand.

THE RABBIT SWUNG THE SWORD . . .

THE IMPOSSIBLE TRICK

Cos leaped out of the way just in time.

Clang! The sword slammed down onto the checkered floor just behind him. Cos scrambled to his feet, ready to dodge another strike.

"**Wait!**" the King's other head said.

The giant rabbit froze, its muscles bulging.

"What are you doing?" the first head demanded.

"Real magic is **dull**," the second head said. "There's no mystery. I know exactly how the spells work. But I enjoyed the trick with the apple. I have no idea how it was done."

Everyone stared at the King, **astonished**.

"I would like to see more illusions," the second head continued. "Flex, put the sword away."

The big rabbit lumbered back up toward the throne.

Hope twinkled in Cos's chest.

"I would be honored to show you more tricks, your majesty," he said.

"Outrageous," grumbled the King's first head.

"Make that clock **disappear**," the second head told Cos. He stood and pointed to an old grandfather clock near the wall. It looked heavy.

Cos blinked. He didn't usually let the audience tell him what to do. But the audience didn't usually threaten to cut his head off, either.

"Certainly, your majesty," he said. "I'll need a dressing room, and a day or two to prepare."

You have ten minutes.

The flicker of hope died.

That's ridiculous. Make it five minutes.

Hollow pushed Cos out of the King's chamber and along a stone corridor toward a dressing room. "You'd better make that clock disappear," he said. "Or else . . ."

"Don't worry," Cos said, although he had no idea how he would perform this trick. "I won't disappoint the King."

"He has given you an **impossible** task," Hollow said. "Only I can **save** you."

"What do you mean?" Cos asked, as they approached a thick wooden door with an iron bolt.

"Tell me where the missing spade is," Hollow said. "Then I'll let you go, and tell the King you escaped."

So this was why Hollow had brought him here. To **force** Cos to tell him where Ace was.

As far as Cos knew, Ace was still **hiding** in the

attic of the Copperpot Theater. "I assumed you caught him," Cos said. "I haven't seen him since you chased him out of my theater."

Hollow opened the wooden door, revealing a cramped room with a dusty rug.

"This is your **last chance**," Hollow said.

Cos shrugged. "Sorry, Mellow Yellow," he said. "I can't help you."

"Fine," Hollow snarled. "You now have four minutes."

HE PUSHED COS INTO THE DRESSING ROOM AND SLAMMED THE DOOR SHUT.

It took a second for Cos's eyes to adjust to the candlelight. There were no windows. He lifted up the rug looking for a trapdoor. There wasn't one. The floor and walls were solid silver. A full-length mirror hung from the back of the door. Cos checked behind it, but found nothing useful. The door was made of thick oak.

Cos was trapped.

He took off his fedora. "Snuggles," he whispered, "I need a way out of here!"

Snuggles popped her head out of the hat. "You're the escape artist," she said. "Not me."

"The door is bolted from the outside. The floor, walls and ceiling are solid metal. It's impossible."

"Well then, I guess you'd better make that clock disappear."

"But that's even more impossible," Cos said. "It looked like it **weighed a ton**. I can't move it, especially not in front of **dozens** of witnesses."

"You're a magician. **Impossible** is your whole thing."

Cos groaned. "You're not helping, Snuggles! I have **less than three minutes** to figure this out."

"Listen to me," Snuggles said urgently. "You don't need to move the clock. You just need to make it *look* like it's gone. That's what an illusion is."

"But how can I . . ." Cos hesitated. The wheels started turning in his mind.

"You're welcome," Snuggles said, and **disappeared** back into the hat.

The Thief of Time

When Hollow opened the door, Cos was standing in the middle of the dressing room. The rug was folded under his arm.

"**Time's up**," Hollow said. "Are you going to tell me where the spade is?"

"And miss my chance to **amaze** the King?" Cos said. "Absolutely not."

He carried the rug down the corridor, back to the King's chamber. The lords and ladies fell silent as he entered. One of the women looked familiar, although Cos couldn't figure out where he had seen her before.

"**Finally!**" one of the King's heads said.

"We were getting bored," the other added.

The King watched as Cos walked over to the clock. He held up the rug like a curtain, concealing the clock from view.

Your majesty, I have for you an illusion called *The Thief of Time.*

"This illusion has never been performed before anywhere in **Magicland.** It is quite **dangerous,** so I suggest everyone stand up there," Cos said, pointing with one hand to the platform near the King's throne.

The lords and ladies hurried over while Cos tried not to look relieved. This trick would only work if everyone watched from the same angle.

"Hurry up," the King said.

"Very well," Cos said. **"Three, two, one!"**

He dropped the rug.

THE GRANDFATHER CLOCK WAS GONE.

The lords and ladies gasped. All four of the King's eyes widened. Even Hollow looked shocked.

"There is no spelldust in the air," Cos pointed out. "No real magic has been used. **No laws have been broken**."

The young woman—the one Cos thought he recognized—began to clap. After a moment, the rest of the audience joined her.

Cos bowed, but **the trick was not yet over**.

MAGIC SECRET UNLOCKED

The clock was hidden **behind the mirror** Cos
had brought from the dressing room. He had
tilted it at an angle so the audience couldn't
see their own reflections. If any of them got
too close, the trick would be ruined.

"But how . . ." the King
began.

"It's one thing to make a
grandfather clock vanish,
your majesty," Cos said.
"But wouldn't it be more
impressive to make a clock
appear out of thin air?"

He held up the rug, knocked over the mirror and dropped the rug on top of it, all in the space of a second. The lords and ladies boggled as the clock reappeared before their eyes.

TA-DA!

Cos sighed with relief. He had done the impossible. When he got back to the Coppertown Theater, he might start work on an improved version of this trick.

"Your majesty," Hollow interrupted, "I have just received word that **Cosentino is hiding your missing soldier**, the Ace of Spades!"

Both of the King's heads spun to look at Cos.

"WHaT?!"

"If he doesn't reveal the soldier's whereabouts," Hollow added, "I would humbly suggest that you kill him."

The giant rabbit, who had been sleeping on the floor, looked up **eagerly**.

"Where is the Ace of Spades?" the King bellowed at Cos.

"I don't know what he's talking about, your majesty," Cos said. "I'm just a simple illusionist from Coppertown."

But the King trusted Hollow.

"OFF WiTH HiS HeaD!"

The giant rabbit stood up and grabbed his sword once again.

"Your majesty," cried a voice.

The King rolled his eyes. "What can I do for you, **Princess Priscilla?**"

Cos looked over. It was the woman who had looked familiar. And suddenly he knew why— she had been in the audience at the Copperpot Theater, wearing the hooded cloak. He recognized her blue eyes. Now she was dressed in a purple dress.

Princess Priscilla was the King's niece. What

PRINCESS PRISCILLA

PRINCESS OF MAGICLAND, SILVER CASTLE, SILVER CITY
ABILITIES: LEVITATION, SWEET, KIND HEART, EXTREMELY CLEVER

had she been doing at Cos's show in Coppertown?

"If you keep the illusionist alive," Priscilla said, "he may change his mind and decide to talk."

"**Silence**," the King said. "I've made my decision."

Priscilla kept talking. Apparently the King couldn't control her. She, like Ace, must not have any evil in her heart.

"Are you sure?" she pressed. "Perhaps you want to consult your other head."

"Actually," the King's other head said, "she makes a good point."

"No she doesn't," the first head grumbled.

"Yes she does. Flex!"

The giant rabbit **huffed**.

"Take the illusionist to . . .

THE ARCADE,"

the King continued.

"The Puzzler can deal with him."

Cos gasped. He didn't want to lose his head by a giant rabbit, but The Arcade might be even **worse**. The lords and ladies looked horrified.

Flex grabbed Cos's collar and **dragged** him out of the chamber. Cos caught Princess Priscilla's eye. He still didn't know why she was trying to save him.

Priscilla mouthed something at him:

Good luck.

Then the doors slammed closed.

The Arcade

Flex pulled Cos down several flights of stairs into darker and darker regions of the castle. Eventually he hauled Cos through an iron door into a cold dungeon.

A stone well with a silver lid stood in the center of the room.

Flex unlocked the heavy lid, and grunted as he lifted it, revealing a circle of pure blackness.

Cos realized what the giant rabbit was about to do. He **struggled** to get free, but it was useless. Flex was too strong.

Instead, Cos shook his head until his hat fell off. The hat hit the floor and rolled into the corner. "Snuggles," Cos hissed. **"Get help!"**

Then Flex **dropped** Cos into the well.

Cos plummeted into the darkness, faster and faster. He shielded his face with his arms as the walls of the well rushed past, scraping his elbows and his bare feet.

There was a *clank* from high above as Flex closed the heavy silver lid, **cutting out all the light**.

Cos had never fallen so far without a safety rope. Unless there was a pile of mattresses at the bottom of the well, he was going to die . . .

Cos slammed onto the stone floor, jarring his knees and shoulders.

But he wasn't dead. He didn't even think he had broken any bones. How was that possible?

WHAM!

OWWW!

Cos clambered to his feet as his eyes adjusted to the gloom. He had landed in a cavern as big as a football field. Someone had filled it with junk—a rusty popcorn machine, a shooting gallery littered with faded toys, an air hockey table with two broken legs. Cobwebs covered a small roller coaster.

The ground under Cos's feet was a papier-mâché of damp cardboard and rotting food. The air was so cold that his breath made clouds around his head.

He turned around slowly. A row of arcade game machines leaned against the wall behind him, their lights occasionally flashing. A metal claw dangled inside a glass box filled with prizes. As Cos watched, a spider crawled out of the coin slot and scuttled away into the darkness.

"Hello?" Cos called again.

His voice echoed around the cavern. There was no response.

A cockroach as big as a phone crawled over Cos's bare foot. He yelped and stumbled back.

Then he heard footsteps, fast and light.

SOMEONE WAS RUNNING TOWARD HiM.

Cos backed away, closer to the game machines. Whoever else was down here, he hoped they were friendly.

A boy appeared from behind the shooting gallery. He had curly brown hair and wore a puffy red vest over a denim jacket. A fluorescent cap was pulled low over his dark eyes. One of his hands was gloved.

Who's there?

The boy didn't look
threatening, so Cos
stepped into view.

"I'm Cos," he said.

The kid ran up to him and
extended his ungloved hand.
"Hey, Cos. What's cooking?"

Cos wasn't sure how to answer that.

"I'm Eighties," the kid continued. "Welcome to
The Arcade."

Cos shook his hand. "Great to meet you, Eighties."

"Come on, I'll show you around."

Cos followed Eighties through the cavern, skirting
around piles of broken carnival equipment.

He saw other prisoners shuffling around in the **gloom**. People who had angered the King. Their clothes had holes in them and didn't fit properly, as though they had been found at the bottom of the junk heap.

One person was curled in a ball on the dirt. An old woman was digging frantically through the garbage, like she'd lost something important. Two men were collecting junk and stuffing it into a bag, but the bag had a hole in it and objects kept falling out.

"Most people sleep over there, in the **jumper castle**," Eighties said, pointing.

"You can get chocolate from the **skill-tester machine**, or make yourself a **corn dog** in that van over there. We have all three food groups—sugar, fat and salt."

Cos didn't think those were the three food groups, but he didn't say so.

A small car **zoomed** out of the darkness, **shooting sparks**. Eighties pulled Cos out of the way just in time. The car sped away.

"You have to be on the lookout for bumper cars down here," Eighties explained. "And wild dogs. And don't eat the cotton candy. It's made of spiderwebs."

"And don't go in the **mirror maze** without nose plugs," Eighties finished. "We use it as a bathroom."

"How long have you been down here?" Cos asked.

"Not sure," Eighties said. "The King cast a spell so **time moves slower** in The Arcade. Or, to think of it another way, it's like the rest of the world ages in dog years."

"I don't understand," Cos said.

"An hour on the surface takes less than ten minutes down here. Flex threw you down the hole, what, two minutes ago?"

"About that."

"So upstairs, fifteen minutes has already gone by. Flex will be back in the King's chamber by now."

"That's why the fall didn't kill me," Cos realized.

"Because **time slowed down** before I landed."

"Now you're getting it," Eighties said. "Flex throws people down the hole every day, mostly Coppertowners who've been caught using magic, but they only land about once a week."

Cos's heart sank as he realized what this meant. Time was rushing past on the surface. If he didn't find a **way out of here** soon, years would pass. His theater would rot. His friends would grow old without him.

"Why are you down here?" Eighties asked.

"What did you do?"

"Well, when Hollow arrested me, I was using a paper clip to escape from a shark tank," Cos said, exaggerating slightly. "**I'm an escape artist**."

Eighties's eyes widened. "Like MacGyver!"

"Like who?"

"So you can pick locks, then?"

Cos shrugged. "Most kinds, sure."

Eighties looked each way, and then leaned closer to Cos. "Follow me," he whispered.

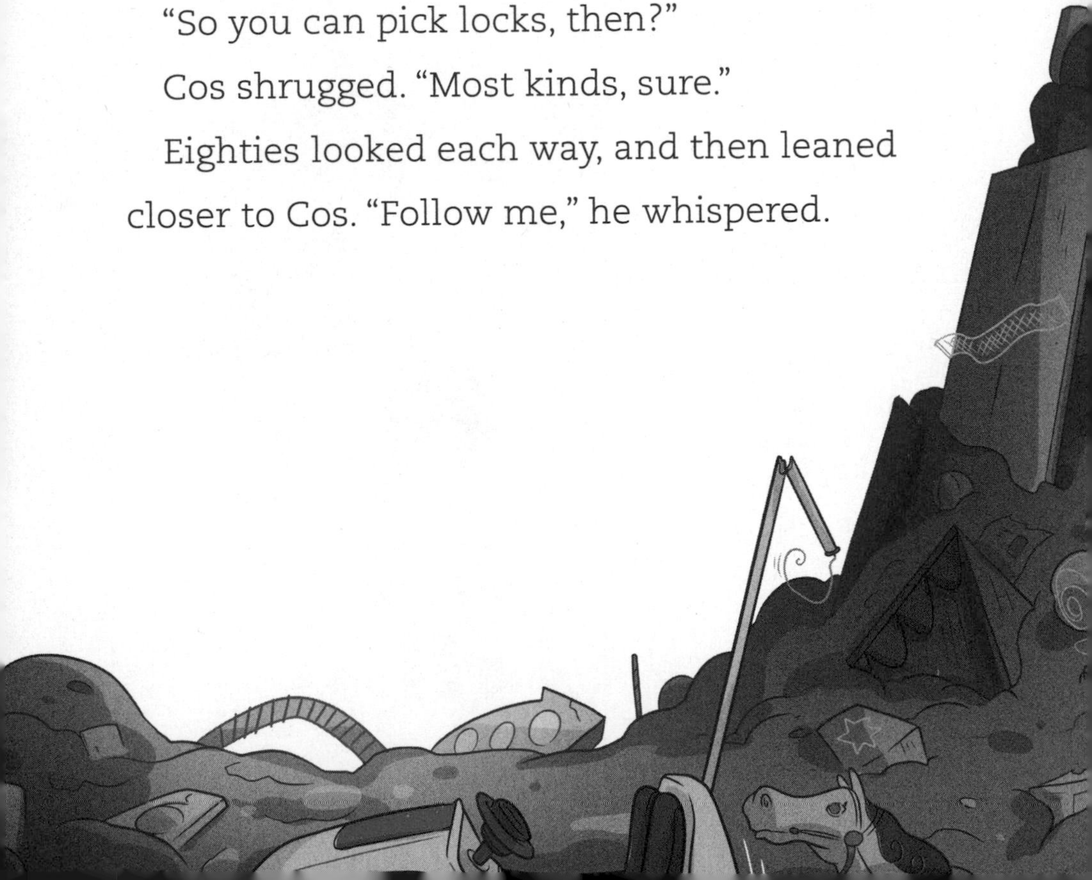

He led Cos deeper into the maze of garbage, away from the sputtering lights of the arcade machines. There were no people around.

"One way out? Is it the well?" Cos guessed.

"No. Even if you could somehow climb it, the lid is always locked. But there are **three doors** at the other end of the cavern. One of them leads outside."

Cos rubbed his hands together. "So what's the problem?"

"**THE PUZZLER**. She guards the doors. She's very loyal to the King and, thanks to her magic, she's **superstrong** and she **can't be hurt**. At least five people have tried to sneak past her to get to the doors. She caught them, and forced them to play a—stop!"

Cos stopped. The path ahead was covered by a damp blanket. Cos wondered if this was where Eighties slept.

"I figure," Eighties continued, "we can lure the

Puzzler away from the doors and trap her."

"How?"

Eighties lifted the corner of the blanket. Cos had assumed there was solid ground underneath, but there was actually a deep pit.

"Puzzler will fall into the pit. It's like the shark

"Puzzler will fall into the pit. It's like the shark tank illusion," Cos said, quickly filling in Eighties on the trick. "Except I didn't fall into the tank because there was something beneath my feet, even though it looked like there wasn't."

"I've been digging for weeks," Eighties said. "She might be able to climb out, but it'll take her a while. Long enough for us to figure out which door is the right one, pick the lock, and get everyone out of The Arcade."

Eighties put the blanket back into position. Once again, it looked like there was solid ground beneath it.

"Do you think you can lure her over the pit?" Cos asked.

Eighties nodded. "She likes games, and she's always looking for new players. Whenever a new prisoner falls down the hole, she goes looking for them. New prisoners are the only ones dumb enough to play."

Cos was about to ask more questions when a voice echoed through The Arcade.

"LADIES and GENTLEMEN, we have a *new* CONTESTANT!"

THE PUZZLER

The color drained from Eighties's face. "That's Puzzler!" he whispered. "Hide!"

Eighties and Cos edged around the blanket and ran farther up the path between two huge piles of garbage.

The booming voice was getting closer behind them. **"STEP RiGHT UP, STEP RiGHT UP!"**

Eighties ducked behind a fallen foosball table. Cos dove sideways into a pile of garbage, digging until he was buried. The smell was terrible.

Footsteps crunched along the alleyway. Cos held his breath.

Puzzler's mad laughter echoed through The Arcade.

"What's this?" she asked. "A picnic blanket! **HOW LOVELY**."

Cos raised his head slightly, risking a peek.

PUZZLER

DUNGEON MASTER AND GAME SHOW HOST,
THE ARCADE, SILVER CITY
ABILITIES: SUPERSTRONG, CAN'T BE HURT,
VERY SMART, A MASTERMIND

Puzzler had a jigsaw piece for a head, and was wearing a striped maroon suit. One of her eyes was focused on the blanket, while the others scanned the junk heaps up ahead.

She reached down toward the blanket with one clawed hand. If she lifted it, she would see the hole. Eighties's trap would be **ruined**. But if she were **distracted** somehow . . .

Cos pushed his way out of the garbage pile. He turned to run, but not too fast. He wanted Puzzler to chase him, so she would fall into the hole.

But Puzzler didn't fall into Eighties's trap. With **superhuman strength** she leaped into the air and soared over the blanket. She crashed to the ground right behind Cos and grabbed his shoulder with a clawed hand.

Cos found himself spun around until he was looking into those rolling eyes staring out of her misshapen head.

"**Aha!**" she cried. "We have a new contestant, ladies and gentlemen!" Puzzler held a microphone in front of Cos's face. "Tell the audience your name and a little bit about yourself."

Her claws were still crushing his shoulder. She was unbelievably strong.

Cos looked around, but he didn't see anyone. Nor were there any cameras. "What audience?" he asked.

"They always hide," Puzzler grumbled. "I don't know why—I put on a great show every time. Come on, tell me your name."

I'm Cosentino, THE GRAND ILLUSIONIST!
A celebrity guest! How exciting! I'M YOUR HOST, PUZZLER!
Here's the deal, Mr. Cosentino. We're going to play a game. If you win, you get to leave The Arcade. You'll be free!

Cos blinked. Was there a way out of The Arcade after all?

"But if you lose," Puzzler continued, "you get eaten by a hungry tiger. What do you say?" Puzzler's laugh was like a rattling drain.

"Don't do it!" Eighties jumped up from behind the foosball table. "No one ever wins her game."

Puzzler's grin grew wider. "That's not true," she said. "I win all the time."

This was probably some kind of trap—but Cos desperately needed to get out of here.

"If you win all the time," he said slowly, "maybe we could raise the stakes a little bit."

Puzzler looked delighted. "We have a gambler, ladies and gentlemen! What did you have in mind, Mr. Cosentino?"

"**IF I WIN,**" Cos said, "**everyone GOES FREE.**"

He heard a sharp intake of breath from the shadows. Apparently other prisoners *were* watching.

"And if you lose?" Puzzler prompted.

"Then I'll get eaten by a tiger," Cos said. "But you'll have an audience, for once. No one will want to miss this show."

He could tell she was a performer, like him. And performers loved audiences. He could see the wheels turning in Puzzler's mind.

"Very well," Puzzler said finally. "Even

THE KING HiMSELF

might come down to see that."

"Let's do a **spellbind**," Cos suggested.

A spellbind was a magic handshake which made it impossible to change your mind.

Puzzler hesitated.

Cos held out a hand. "I'll play your game," he said. "And you'll get an amazing show."

Puzzler took his hand in her claw. "And **if** you survive," she said, "everyone goes free."

Magic tingled from Cos's heart into his arm, and then down into his fingertips. **Puzzler's claw started to glow as the spellbind took effect.**

Cos had hardly ever used magic since the King had banned it. His spell book rarely ever left his attic. He had forgotten how good it felt to unleash his real powers.

"NO!" Eighties cried.

But Cos didn't get the chance to reassure him.
Puzzler lifted Cos up with her incredible strength,
and carried him deeper into the darkness of

THE ARCADE.

SPELLBOUND

Puzzler carried Cos over to one of the fairground attractions—a ride designed to lift people up high and then drop them down at **terrifying speeds**. Fortunately, it was switched off.

Puzzler pushed Cos into one of the seats and buckled him in. Then she waved a hand at the harness, casting a spell. A flash of light exploded from her fingers. The harness tightened across Cos's chest, and the buckle transformed into

a HUGE

COMBINATION LOCK.

Spelldust rained down on Cos's head.

"I promised to play your game," Cos said. "I'm spellbound. **You don't need to lock me up.**"

"Just a precaution," Puzzler said. "Don't go anywhere, we'll be back right after these messages."

Then she walked away into the shadows.

Cos immediately got to work. He had agreed to

play the game, but that didn't mean he had to stay in this chair. He needed to prepare.

There were fifty notches on the dial of the lock. The combination was probably at least three numbers long, so there were more than a hundred thousand possible combinations. He would have to **hurry**.

He rotated the dial, trying to feel the clicks.

"You're crazy."

Cos looked up. Eighties was standing nearby, looking awed.

"Probably," Cos admitted. "You'd better tell me how the game works."

Eighties sat in the chair next to him. "It's pretty simple. There are three doors. One leads out of The Arcade. The other two have tigers behind them."

"And I get to pick one?" Cos asked.

"Right."

"And then what happens?"

"And then you get **eaten** by a tiger. No one has ever picked the right door."

A sense of doom settled over Cos. Puzzler had promised to let everyone out if he survived— but she hadn't promised that it was possible to survive. There were probably tigers behind all three doors. He was as good as dead.

"Cos!" A familiar figure was running through The Arcade toward him. It was Ace, the missing spade!

"Ace!" Cos said. "What are you doing here?"

"I'm busting you out," Ace said. "Professor Camouflage is upstairs with a rope, holding the well lid open, and Locki's waiting outside with a getaway cart. After you'd been missing for a few days, I started working on an escape plan."

"A few *days*?" Cos said. "I only just got here!"

"Time runs slower down here," Eighties reminded him.

Ace noticed Eighties for the first time. "Who's this?"

Before Eighties could reply, Professor Camouflage appeared. "Ace!" he said. "Where have you been? We've been waiting for hours!"

"Hours?" Ace said. "I've only just gotten here!"

"Time runs slower down here," Eighties said again.

"Who's this?" the Professor asked, pointing at Eighties.

Locki appeared behind the Professor. "Hey!" he said. "What's the holdup? I was waiting outside for ages!"

"I only just got here!" the Professor said.

"Me too," Ace said.

Eighties buried his face in his hands. "Time runs slower down here!"

"Hey, who's this?" Locki said.

"Everyone just be quiet for a second," Cos said. "Locki, can you get me out of this thing?"

Locki started fiddling with the combination lock. He worked so fast the dial was a blur.

"Done!" Locki said. The combination lock popped open.

Cos stood up. "Thanks, Locki."

"But I can't leave," Cos told the others. "I'm spellbound. And there are lots of other people down here who need help."

"The getaway cart only has six seats," Ace said. "Plus the driver."

Cos gritted his teeth. There had to be a way to save the other prisoners.

An idea jumped into his head. It was dangerous. Maybe deadly. But it was his only shot.

"ACE—DO YOU KNOW ANYTHING ABOUT TIGER TAMING?"

THREE-DOOR MONTE

"Ladies and gentlemen," Puzzler yelled.

"It's time to play

THREE-DOOR MONTE!"

She waited for applause. There was none.

Cos was standing on a concrete stage, his ankles chained together.

Behind him was a brick wall with three locked doors, their doorknobs painted velvety red.

In front of him was a crowd of prisoners, sitting on rusty metal chairs. Cos had promised Puzzler an audience, and he had delivered. Everyone wanted to see if he could win them their freedom.

Eighties was in the front row, nervously twisting the sides of a colored toy cube.

Puzzler stood beside Cos, her clawed hand on his shoulder. If he tried to run, he wouldn't get far.

Cos could hear a low growling sound coming from behind one of the doors, but he couldn't tell which one.

"In that case," Cos said, "I'm feeling good."
He hoped his plan would work.

With an explosion of spelldust,
the King appeared, lounging
on his throne in the
middle of the
audience.

Hollow stood on one side of him, and Princess Priscilla stood on the other.

"Your majesty!" Puzzler bowed. "I'm honored that you could be here."

One of the King's heads looked around at the prisoners with great disdain.

What is that smell?

"It's the smell of *excitement*, your majesty," Puzzler said. "I was just about to explain how the game worked."

She waved her hand toward the three doors. "First, the contestant will choose a door. One of the doors leads to freedom. But the—"

"Perhaps his majesty would like to see an illusion first," Cos interrupted.

"**Yes!**" said one of the King's heads. "I like illusions!"

 "**NO!**" said the other at the same moment.

Puzzler frowned. "The King is here to watch my game."

"I would like to see a trick," Priscilla said.

Cos didn't give them the opportunity to keep arguing. He hopped away from the three doors and pulled two playing cards from his pocket. The spotlight followed him.

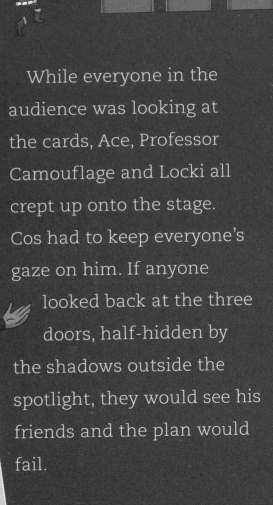

While everyone in the audience was looking at the cards, Ace, Professor Camouflage and Locki all crept up onto the stage. Cos had to keep everyone's gaze on him. If anyone looked back at the three doors, half-hidden by the shadows outside the spotlight, they would see his friends and the plan would fail.

"I have in my hand," Cos said, "two cards." He showed the faces. "The King of Diamonds . . ." he nodded to the King, ". . . and the Ace of Spades."

Priscilla and Flex gasped. The King glared. "Is this a joke?" he demanded.

"Not at all, your majesty," Cos said. "It's a magic trick. Don't take your eyes off the cards because one of them is about to **disappear**."

He heard the faintest click as Locki opened door number three. Professor Camouflage and Ace should be slipping inside right now. Cos had to keep the audience distracted long enough for Locki to close the door and get off the stage.

Cos turned the cards so only the King of Diamonds was visible.

The audience watched closely.

"Now, with a snap of my fingers . . ."

Cos clicked his fingers and turned both cards around so the audience could see.

BOTH CARDS WERE NOW THE KING OF DIAMONDS.

"The Ace of Spades has vanished!" Cos declared.

He could see the audience frowning, trying to figure out what he had done. Behind him, he heard Locki slip off the stage.

"Fear not, your majesty," Cos said quickly. "It's right here in my pocket." He reached into his pocket and pulled out the Ace of Spades.

"OUTRAGEOUS!"

Like all the best tricks, it was as simple as it was impossible. The audience of prisoners—already locked up with nothing to fear from the King—burst into rapturous applause.

"KiLL HiM!" the King screamed.

Puzzler grinned madly. "Don't worry, sire. He'll never survive the game."

She grabbed Cos by the throat and lifted him off his feet. Cos felt his eyes bulging. Not enough blood was getting to his brain.

"Number three," Cos croaked.

Puzzler dragged him over to door number three and put him down. It was a thick door, but Cos thought he could hear scuffling noises and chains rattling inside. It sounded like Ace and the Professor were still trying to control the tiger.

"Before I open this door," Puzzler said, "I'm going to do you a little favor."

"No!" the King shouted. "No favors!"

"I beg your indulgence, your majesty," Puzzler said.

She walked over to a different door—door number two. She pushed the key into the lock, and twisted.

The door creaked open . . .

There was silence for a moment. Then something snarled from the blackness beyond.

Yellow eyes gleamed. There was a flash of white fur and claws, and suddenly a huge tiger was sprinting toward the doorway, teeth bared.

Puzzler closed the door just in time. The tiger slammed into the other side, scrabbling at the wood.

Cos's heart was pounding. That tiger had been **huge**. If it got loose, he would be dead in seconds.

"I'm going to give you another chance," Puzzler told Cos. "Would you like to change your mind?"

"Not to *that* door," Cos said.

There was nervous laughter in the crowd.

"No?" Puzzler walked over to door number one. "How about this one?"

"I'll stick with door **number three**."

"When you picked that door, you only had a one in three chance of getting it right. Therefore there's a two in three chance that door number one leads to freedom. Wouldn't you agree?"

Cos wouldn't be tricked. "Door number three," he said.

Puzzler's smile broadened. Cos wondered if he had made a terrible mistake.

"Very well," she said. "Ladies and gentlemen, shall we see if he's won?"

Silence from the crowd.

Cos held his breath.

PUZZLER WALKED OVER TO DOOR NUMBER THREE.

INSERTED THE KEY . . .

UNLOCKED THE DOOR . . .

PULLED IT OPEN . . .

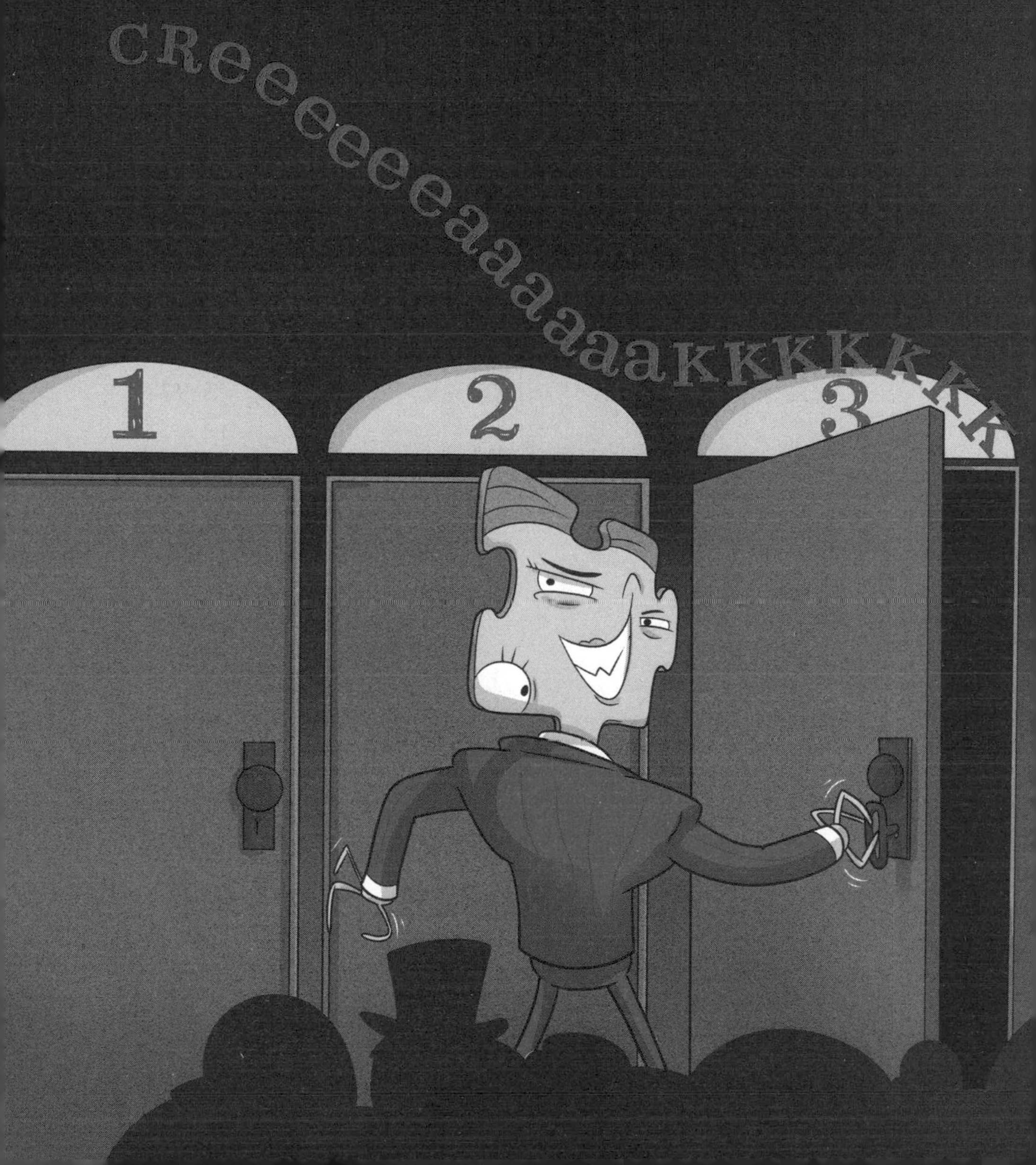

A HUGE

TIGER

SPRINTED

OUT OF THE

SHADOWS.

TIGER UNLEASHED

Cos scrambled backward, the chains rattling around his ankles. Someone in the audience screamed. Puzzler laughed hysterically.

The tiger exploded through the doorway. It leaped toward Cos, claws outstretched. Its teeth were as big as ice picks.

"**Sleep**," Cos shouted.

The tiger faltered. It stared at Cos with suspicious yellow eyes.

"Sleep," Cos said again, putting on his best hypnosis voice. He held out a hand and lowered it slowly.

The tiger sat down like an obedient dog.

"Roy! What are you doing?" Puzzler screeched

The tiger ignored them—
because it wasn't a real
tiger. It was Professor
Camouflage!

The real tiger was
still in the darkness
behind the door,
trapped in a cage Ace
had made.

"Sleep," Cos said,
scratching the fake
tiger under the chin.
"Good kitty."

The tiger stretched
its legs and tail. Then it
curled up and closed its
eyes.

Puzzler stared at it, horrified. "**ROY! wake up!**"

The tiger didn't move.

Cos looked back at the prisoners. Amazement lit up their faces.

"Wow!" Cos said. "**I won!**"

"No, you didn't," Puzzler said. "You picked the wrong door."

"If I survive, everyone goes free," Cos said. "That was the deal. You're **spellbound**."

"You cheated," Puzzler snarled.

"Did I?" Cos said. "Perhaps you could open door number one? Then we'll see who cheated."

Puzzler hesitated. Cos had suspected all along that there were tigers behind all three doors.

That was how Puzzler always won the game, until now. She couldn't open the door without revealing the truth.

"This isn't over, Mr. Cosentino," she hissed.

Cos thought about the evil King and his unfair laws. He had stolen magic from the people, and imprisoned anyone who tried to get it back.

"No," Cos said. "It isn't."

"DON'T YOU DARE LET HIM GO!" the King yelled.

But Puzzler had no choice. It was impossible to go back on a spellbind. She raised her hand.

"Hollow!" the King yelled. "Grab him!"

Hollow leaped up onto the stage. But he was too late. Puzzler snapped her fingers—

and there was an explosion of spelldust and a blinding light.

Home Sweet Home

When Cos opened his eyes, he was outside. The sun was warm on his face. He and all the other prisoners—including Eighties, Locki and Ace—were standing outside Coppertown.

He was home.

Eighties was dancing with excitement. He moonwalked, ran on the spot and jerked his arms around like a robot.

"I'm back in Coppertown!" Eighties cried. He thumped Cos on the arm.

"WICKED! RADICAL! SICK!"

Cos assumed those were good words. "You're welcome," he said.

"You nailed it!" Locki said to Cos. "We walked right across the stage without anyone noticing— just because you were doing the **Quick Change Card routine!**"

Cos hugged him. "You got that door open so fast that I hardly needed to do anything," he said. "Thank you."

"Thank Ace, not me," said Locki. "The tiger ran at us as soon as we opened the door—but Ace made that cage appear so quickly that it didn't have a chance to eat us."

Ace shrugged modestly. "It was the least I could do," he said. "You guys saved my life from those snakes."

"I actually pushed you into the snake pit," Cos pointed out.

"Yeah, but you got me out again."

Spelldust swirled down out of the sky. A sound like wind chimes echoed through the street.

Cos stepped back just in time. Princess Priscilla appeared in the rain of spelldust. In her glamorous clothes, she looked very out of place in the dusty Coppertown street.

Cos bowed. "Princess."

"Mr. Cosentino," Priscilla said. "That was quite a show."

"Why did you help me?" Cos asked.

Priscilla smiled. "Not everyone in Silver City is selfish," she said. "Some of us want Magicland to be fair."

Cos took a risk. "Your uncle doesn't seem interested in fairness."

"No," Priscilla agreed. "You've made a **powerful enemy**."

"Cos!"

Cos turned around in time to see a monkey running toward him.

"Professor," Cos said. "Did you have any trouble climbing out of the well?"

The monkey transformed into Professor Camouflage.

"We have a big problem," he said. "The King's army is coming."

A chill ran up Cos's spine. He turned to look at the horizon. Dozens of soldiers were marching in the distance, getting closer and closer. Hollow was in the lead. Flex was right beside him.

"What do we do?" Locki asked.

Cos looked around. All the former prisoners were watching him. Waiting for advice.

"We disappear," Cos said.

You can learn Cos's trick from page 161!

QUICK CHANGE CARDS
MAGIC TRICK INSTRUCTIONS

REQUIRED ITEMS:

An Ace of Spades

A King of Diamonds

A trick card: An Ace of Spades with a King of Diamonds on the reverse side.

TIP: to make your own trick card, glue two standard Ace of Spades and King of Diamonds playing cards together.

SETUP: Put the Ace of Spades in your pocket.

METHOD: Hold the other 2 cards in your right hand with the trick card on top, with the Ace of Spades facing upward. Show the cards as one, front and back, to your spectator (**FiG. 1**), and say, "I have the Ace of Spades in my hand."

TiP: the back of the King will appear to be the back of the trick Ace.

FiG. 2

While keeping the Ace of Spades facing forward, slip the King of Diamonds out from behind it, into your left hand and show it, front and back, to your spectator (**FiG. 2**). Say, "And here is the King of Diamonds." Then say, "Now I am going to make the Ace of Spades disappear! Are you watching closely?"

With an immediate action, turn over the King of Diamonds and place it on top of the trick Ace of Spades card and then turn the two cards over with your right hand as you say, "The Ace of Spades has changed into the King of Diamonds!" (**FiG. 3–7**).

FiG. 3

FiG. 4

FiG. 5

FiG. 6

FiG. 7

Your spectator will be amazed that the Ace of Spades has turned into the King of Diamonds in front of their eyes!

With that, take out the Ace of Spades from your pocket and say, "Fear not! The Ace of Spades is right here in my pocket!" (**FiG. 8**).

FiG. 8

COSENTINO is now regarded as one of the world's leading magicians and escape artists. He is a multiple winner of the prestigious Merlin Award (the Oscar for international magicians) and is the highest-selling live act in his home country, Australia.

Cosentino's four prime-time TV specials have aired in over 40 countries and he has toured his award-winning live shows to full houses across the world.

JACK HEATH is a bestselling, award-winning Australian author of thrillers and used to be a street magician!

JAMES HART is an Australian children's illustrator who has illustrated many books.

Photo credit: Pierre Baroni

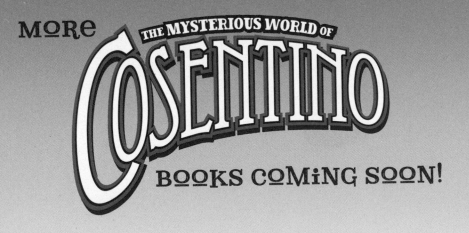

MORE **THE MYSTERIOUS WORLD OF COSENTINO** BOOKS COMING SOON!